GIGANTOSAURUS

**For Daisy and Rosie – always follow your own path
and don't listen to boneheads! Love, Daddy xx**

A TEMPLAR BOOK

First published in the UK in 2014 by Templar Publishing
This softback edition published in 2014 by Templar Publishing,
an imprint of The Templar Company Limited,
Deepdene Lodge, Deepdene Avenue, Dorking, Surrey, RH5 4AT, UK
www.templarco.co.uk

ISBN 978-1-78370-051-6

Edited by Libby Hamilton

Printed in Turkey

GIGANTOSAURUS

by Jonny Duddle

templar publishing

Many million years ago,

beyond the path of the lava flow,

on the edge of the jungle, where the herbivores grazed,
four little dinosaurs spent their days
playing in the Cretaceous sun,
following tracks and having fun.

The dinosaur mums said:

Beware my child...

... of the **GIGANTOSAURUS,** so FIERCE and WILD!

With teeth as long
as you are tall,
he'd soon make a snack
of one so small.

His feet go STOMP!
His jaws go CRUNCH!
In the blink of an eye
you'd be his LUNCH!

Bonehead, Tiny,
Fin and Bill
went off to play
up on the hill.
The Gigantosaurus
was on their minds
till Bonehead said:

I think you'll find...
we need a lookout and I'm the BEST!
I'll get a good view from that termite nest.

But it was only a minute before
Bonehead cried:

It's the
GIGANTOSAURUS!

Quick!
RUN and HIDE!

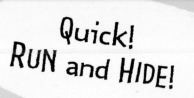

THUD
THUD
THUD

They ran!
They hid!
They shook with fear!
The GIGANTOSAURUS
was coming near!

But there was no STOMP.
There was no CRUNCH.
No fierce monster
had smelled his lunch...

"It's just
TRICERATOPS!"
Bonehead laughed.
"You ran! You hid!
You're all so
DAFT!"

Hello Dad...

Hello Son.

"But you passed
my Emergency Warning Trial.
Now I think I'll keep watch
from that rock awhile."

But a little bit later, Bonehead cried:

The GIGANTOSAURUS!
Quick – RUN and HIDE!

BOM BOM BOM BOM

They ran! They hid!
They shook with fear!

The GIGANTOSAURUS
was coming near!

But there was no STOMP.
There was no CRUNCH.
No hungry beast after snacks to munch...

"It's old DIPLODOCUS!"
Bonehead laughed.

"You ran! You hid!
You're all so daft!"

"But danger lurks,
as you need to learn.
I'll look out from that
enormous fern."

It didn't take long
till they heard a shout...

GIGANTOSAURUS!
You'd better WATCH OUT!

THUMP THUMP THUMP

They RAN! They HID!
They shook with fear!
The GIGANTOSAURUS
was coming near!

But there was no STOMP.
There was no CRUNCH.
No carnivore with a
whiff of lunch...

"It's STEGOSAURUS!"
Bonehead laughed.
"You ran! You hid!
You're all so DAFT!"

"But at least
you've passed my final test.
Now I'm going for a nap
in that comfy nest."

Then, seconds later,
the cry began...

GIGANTOSAURUS!
Run as fast as you can!

But though his friends heard
what Bonehead cried,
by now they knew
that Bonehead lied.

"That's it!" said Bill.
"We're off to explore.
And we're not going to
play with YOU
ANYMORE."

No one left to trick, Bonehead was alone.
He began to wish he was back home.
For an awful noise was coming near,
and now there WAS good reason for fear...

The feet went

STOMP!

But then they heard
a muffled cry
from the scraps
of nest that
lay nearby...

I'm here!
It's ME! I HAVE survived!
I'm sorry that I tricked and lied.
But this time, honestly, it's true –
there's a PTERODACTYL
after you!

game.

And though Bonehead thought they'd run in fright,
his friends just shrugged and said,
"Yeah, right!"

MEET THE DINOSAURS IN THIS BOOK...

PARASAUROLOPHUS
Palaeontologists* think this dinosaur's large crest was used to make sounds!

TRICERATOPS
This dinosaur had a huge skull – 1/3 the length of its whole body.

ANKYLOSAURUS
A full-grown adult weighed as much as 5 or 6 tonnes!

STEGOSAURUS
This dinosaur's spiked tail is called a thagomizer.

*Palaeontologist: a scientist who studies prehistoric times.

BRACHIOSAURUS

A truly huge herbivore, Tiny's mum will grow to be even bigger than Diplodocus!

DIPLODOCUS

This giant dinosaur had a comically tiny brain.

PTERODACTYL

There's no such thing as a pterodactyl, but that's what most people call pterosaurs (flying lizards). What Bonehead meant to say was pteranodon, or more specifically quetzalcoatlus, but he couldn't pronounce that.

GIGANTOSAURUS
This scary dinosaur was
made up for this book!*

*But there was a dinosaur a lot like this one, called Gigan_o_tosaurus.
It was the largest-known theropod (meat-eaters that stood on two legs),
bigger even than a tyrannosaurus rex.

Gigantosaurus was a name given to some scattered dinosaur bones
found by early palaeontologists in England and Africa. But it was all such a
muddle that science has never used the name since.

THE END